FAT, FAT
ROSE MARIE

FAT, FAT ROSE MARIE

written and illustrated by

LISA PASSEN

Henry Holt and Company • New York

First edition
Published by Henry Holt and Company, Inc.,
115 West 18th Street, New York, New York 10011.
Published simultaneously in Canada by Fitzhenry & Whiteside Ltd.,
195 Allstate Parkway, Markham, Ontario L3R 4T8.

Library of Congress Cataloging-in-Publication Data
Passen, Lisa.
Fat, fat Rose Marie / written and illustrated by Lisa Passen.
Summary: A little girl must stand up to the class bully who keeps
picking on her overweight friend.
ISBN 0-8050-1653-8
[1. Friendship—Fiction.   2. Weight control—Fiction.   3. Bullies—
Fiction.]   I. Title.
PZ7.P26937Fat   1991
[E]—dc20   90-21112

Henry Holt books are available at special discounts
for bulk purchases for sales promotions, premiums,
fund-raising, or educational use. Special editions
or book excerpts can also be created to specification.

Printed in the United States of America
on acid-free paper.∞

1   3   5   7   9   10   8   6   4   2

Dedicated to my brother Joe

Rose Marie was the new girl in our class. Miss Binn, our teacher, introduced her to us one morning. "Girls and boys, say hello to Rose Marie. She is a new student at Central Avenue Elementary School."

Rose Marie smiled and said, "Hello!"

Rose Marie had the shiniest blond hair and the biggest blue eyes I had ever seen. She was also . . . well . . . she was kind of . . .

"Fat, fat Rose Marie!" sang Genevieve from the back row. All the kids around her laughed—just like when they laugh at my freckles and red hair. I didn't laugh at Rose Marie.

Later, in gym class, Rose Marie and I were standing alone, waiting to be picked for dodgeball. I am usually the last girl to be picked for a team. Rose Marie whispered to me, "I don't care what side I'm on, but I hope we're on the same team. What's your name?"

"Claire," I replied.

"Why don't we sit together at lunch, Claire?"

Rose Marie and I sat at the last table in the cafeteria. She told me that she had a dog named Buttons. I told her that I didn't have a dog, but that I had a little brother named Harry.

I asked Rose Marie to come over to my house to play after school. She said yes, but she would have to tell her mother first.

Genevieve and her friends were giggling and pointing at us all during lunchtime. I never liked Genevieve much.

That afternoon Rose Marie and I played dolls in my room. Then we colored. I told Rose Marie coloring was my favorite thing to do.

Rose Marie said that her favorite thing to do was play Movie Stars. "How do you play Movie Stars?" I asked.

"Well," she said with deep thought. "We need some grown-up clothes and some lipstick and a hairbrush, to start with."

I asked my mother, and she let us use some of her old things. Playing Movie Stars really was a lot of fun!

"I'm Jean Harlow and you're Rita Hayworth," said Rose Marie, posing in front of a full-length mirror.

"Jean who?" I asked with my most perfect Movie Star expression.

"Doesn't matter," she replied. "Let's accept our Academy Awards!"

Soon it was time to say good-bye. I had had a lot of fun playing with Rose Marie. I liked her a lot, and I thought she liked me. Usually it's hard for me to make friends. I get scared and don't talk much. But with Rose Marie I could talk and talk and talk!

As Rose Marie walked away, I saw Genevieve and her friends down the street.

"Fat, fat Rose Marie! Fattest girl I ever did see!" they shouted.

Rose Marie looked down at the ground and said nothing. I closed the door.

After school the next day, I went to play at Rose Marie's house. "This is my Buttons!" said Rose Marie, holding her dog.

"Hi, Buttons," I said quietly. "Do you think he'll let me pet him?"

"Of course you can pet Buttons!" said Rose Marie's mom. "He doesn't bite. You don't have to be afraid of him, Claire."

Rose Marie's mom was real nice.

We worked on our math and studied our spelling. I was good at spelling, but I was not so good at math. Rose Marie was very, very good at math, and she helped me with my homework.

"See?" said Rose Marie, explaining with her pencil. "It's not so hard, is it?" And it wasn't so hard after all!

We played catch with Buttons, and then Rose Marie showed me some tricks she had taught him. "Speak! Roll over! Jump! Lie down!"

When it was time to go home, Rose Marie and I promised to play again tomorrow.

That's how it was every day. Rose Marie and I would walk to school together and play at recess together and walk home together and do our homework together. I really liked being with Rose Marie.

But every day Genevieve would call her "fat, fat Rose Marie."

I didn't think that was very nice, but I didn't say anything.

One morning Miss Binn announced that we would be going to a carnival for our class trip.

"Wow!" exclaimed Rose Marie. "That's going to be a lot of fun!"

"It sure will!" I said.

"Do they have a sideshow at the carnival?" asked Genevieve. "You know . . . like with a FAT lady?"

Miss Binn gave Genevieve a stern look. "No, Genevieve," she replied. "I do not believe they have a sideshow."

Rose Marie and I looked forward to the carnival all week. When the day came, we sat together on the school bus.

"I want to go on the merry-go-round and the roller coaster! What do you want to go on?" Rose Marie asked me. "I want to go in the fun house!" I said. "The fun house is exciting!" said Rose Marie. "But it's dark and scary, too, so we'll have to make sure we hold on to each other when we go!"

Our bus pulled into the carnival parking lot. It was wonderful! There were rides and games and balloons, and booths selling hot dogs and cotton candy, and music was playing!

Miss Binn gave each of us a handful of tickets as we got off the bus, and told us what time to be back by.

Rose Marie took my hand, and we ran over to the water-gun-burst-the-balloon game. I pulled the trigger while Rose Marie aimed—and we won! We picked a stuffed dinosaur as our prize and named him Boris.

Next we went on the merry-go-round. I had a yellow horse with pale-blue eyes, and Rose Marie had a violet horse that looked like it was singing.

"Boris is having fun!" shouted Rose Marie, and we both laughed.

We got in the line for the roller coaster. Genevieve was already there. She looked at us and made a face.

"Oh, no!" exclaimed Genevieve. "It's fat, fat Rose Marie! She's going to get on this ride and break the ride and we're all going to DIE!"

That was the silliest thing I'd ever heard.

"Nobody can get on any ride with Rose Marie!" shouted Genevieve. "Nobody! She's too fat, and she's got to go on the rides all by herself!"

Genevieve grabbed my arm.

"And that includes you, Claire! NOBODY goes on ANY ride with Rose Marie!"

All the kids were staring at me. I felt real funny. I don't know why, but I started to walk away with Genevieve.

As I did, Rose Marie handed me our stuffed dinosaur. "You take care of Boris, Claire," she said.

What was I doing? I hated Genevieve! But I walked away with her anyway.

"You sit right next to ME on the roller coaster, Claire!" gloated Genevieve as she stared at Rose Marie. I did. And Rose Marie sat alone.

I went on the giant swing
sitting next to Genevieve.
And Rose Marie sat alone.
"What a pretty dinosaur you have,
Claire!" said Genevieve with a smirk.
"Can I play with him later?"

I said nothing.

Then we got in line for the fun house. I thought of Rose Marie telling me how dark and scary the fun house was. She was ahead of me in line. She looked real sad. I held Boris tightly.

Genevieve pointed and said, "Look at old fat, fat Rose Marie! Hi ya, slim!" She started to laugh.

For a moment I just stared at Genevieve. And then I did something that I hoped my mother would not get too upset over.

I took the double-scoop French-vanilla ice-cream cone with chocolate sprinkles that Genevieve was licking out of her hand and stuck it in her face!

"You're not a nice person, Genevieve!" I shouted.

Maybe I hadn't been a very nice person either. I ran over to Rose Marie just as she was getting in the car for the fun house.

"Can I go on this ride with you, Rose Marie?" I asked. I was a little afraid of what she might say to me.

Rose Marie smiled and said, "Sure!"

The fun house was scary, but so, so much fun!
Rose Marie and I went on the rest of the rides together.
We even went on the merry-go-round two more times!
It was truly a day to remember!

And you know what? At school the next day, when Genevieve laughed and shouted, "Fat, fat Rose Marie!" not all of the kids laughed along with her. Some of them even sat with us at lunch. And played with us at recess.

Rose Marie and I made lots of friends after that week.
But Rose Marie was always my BEST FRIEND of all!